6TH GRADE REVENGERS
3

A
GAME
— OF —
THORNS

D1060034

STEVEN WHIBLEY

Published by Steven Whibley Publishing
Victoria, British Columbia
www.stevenwhibley.com

Publisher: Steven Whibley
Copyediting: Chandler Groover
Cover Design: Pintado (rogerdespi.8229@gmail.com)

Library and Archives Canada Cataloguing in Publication

Whibley, Steven, 1978-, author
        A game of thorns / Steven Whibley.

(6th grade revengers ; 3)
Issued in print and electronic formats.
ISBN 978-1-927905-12-8 (paperback).--ISBN 978-1-927905-11-1 (pdf)

        I. Title.

PS8645.H46G36 2016   jC813'.6   C2016-904900-0
                                                       C2016-904901-9

For Isaiah, Aubree and Everett

CHAPTER ONE

*T*hree... two... one...

"Now!" Marcus said.

Nothing happened. I sat down on the bus stop bench and shook my head.

Marcus groaned, plopped onto the bench beside me and started muttering angrily. "He should be running out of there by now." A few seconds later the fire alarm went off in the flower shop across the street.

"Why's the fire alarm going off," I asked. "I thought just the sprinkler would go off, not the fire alarm."

Marcus didn't answer. His gaze fixated on the shop across the street. "C'mon, c'mon," he urged.

Just then, Mr. Lee jogged out of the store, soaked and red-in-the-face angry with a potted plant in his hands, like he'd just recued it from the flood.

Marcus stood up. "Ha! It worked. It actually worked. I need to work on my timing." Marcus nodded at the store across the street from us. "But other than that—one more job completed." He dusted off his hands.

"The alarm," I said. "There's no fire in there. We didn't actually start a fire so why's the alarm going off?"

Marcus shrugged. "I dunno. Who cares? Point is, it worked. We are geniuses."

I stood up beside him and elbowed him in the side. "If the alarm is going off, someone's going to call the fire department. If someone calls the fire department then they're going to send fire trucks."

Marcus turned to me and gave me a "So what?" face.

"C'mon," I said. "We're targeting specific people. I don't want the fire department to send trucks to one of our jobs, and then have a real fire to break out across town and we're the reason the trucks couldn't get there."

Marcus scratched his neck and then bobbed his head a bit. "Okay, yeah, good point. We didn't do enough research on that part. But I'm sure the fire department isn't going to come. Probably just a plumber. Don't worry about it."

I listened and didn't hear any sirens in the distance, and a few people had stopped, and seemed to be asking Mr. Lee what was going on. No one seemed alarmed or panicked. I let myself believe Marcus was right and sighed. "I still can't believe that it actually worked." I sat back down on the bench. "The things you can learn on the net, right? I almost don't blame my parents for trying to block me from certain websites."

Marcus laughed. "There isn't a parental block on the planet that can stop me." He jabbed me in the arm. "Oh, and speaking of useful stuff online, I had an awesome idea last night. Picture this," he held up his hands like he was a movie-writer pitching a blockbuster idea. "A website dedicated to all things hacking. And I don't mean, like, computer hacking. I mean world hacking. Like how to wreak havoc in shopping centers, and..." he gestured across the street at Mr. Lee's flower shop, "how to use oven-cleaner to rig an industrial fire sprinkler to go off."

"I'll give you credit for the fire sprinkler," I said, "that was pretty genius. But what do you know about world-hacking, or... wreaking havoc? Who even says *wreaking havoc*?"

Marcus had been my best friend forever, and it was pretty much a draw as far as which of us got the other one into more trouble. But he was also my partner in our Revenger business. Essentially we were fixers—people came to us with problems and we fixed them. Have a crappy boss? A bully at school? A dog that tries to bite you every day on your way home? A sadistic teacher whose power-tripping is making your life miserable? We're the guys who can take care of those things—for a price.

Mr. Lee, it turned out, was a problem for a number of people. In fact, we'd received three requests to take him out. And the reasons behind two of the requests were as clear as the glass vases in his shop.

The first request was from a group of kids who wanted him to pay for selling them flowers that died really quick. Mother's Day presents, they'd said, that had wilted before they'd even had a chance to give them to their moms. That request wasn't enough on its own. Mr. Lee's shop had a reputation that wasn't exactly stellar, but Revengers are a business and I was pretty sure the kids who'd wrote us the letter wanted to pay us in Pokémon cards. Plus, they sounded kinda whiny and Revengers didn't do whiny.

Marcus didn't agree with me at first and thought being a florist was reason enough to take him down. "A service to guys everywhere," he said, joking. "No more wasting money on things that cost a fortune and die days after you buy them."

Eventually he came around to my way of thinking. We needed jobs that paid actual money.

Marcus plopped himself on the bench beside me. "My world-hacking website is going to be awesome. I have it all planned out. It's going to be one mega site." He tugged at the collar of his t-shirt and fanned his face. "Hey, do you want me to make the hacker site part of our Revenger site? If we do it right it could be a kind of one-stop-shop for all things anarchy."

I shook my head. "Let's keep the Revenger site basic, okay? Just keep the form people fill out to tell us about their problem, and the button for payments. We don't want to add stuff that might get traced back to us."

"Traced back to us?" Marcus asked. "Trust me, that's not going to happen. Anyone digs into our site and they'll think we're from a tiny village in Malaysia."

I had no idea how in the world Marcus did what he did, and he always joked that I was clueless—but really, I was only clueless compared to Marcus. What I knew about computers was pretty much what any other eleven-year-old knew. Marcus just happened to be born into a house of computer nerds. Plus, I was pretty sure he had a knack for them that went a bit beyond the stuff his parents taught him. He'd been making websites since he was old enough to grab a keyboard. His dad was a programmer and his mom worked in internet marketing. But despite having a whack of websites, only a couple of Marcus's sites had ever made him any money, and our Revenger site was quickly becoming the most popular.

We had been saving the money for spy camp, but lately we'd shelved that plan and instead put the money back into our growing business.

He pointed at me. "Hey, what if we called ourselves Anarchy Revengers or Anarchy Revengers for Hire?"

"We're already the Revengers. We have a website and a logo and a slogan. Let's just leave it alone. Besides, how are you going to pull all the stuff from all those sites into one place? Won't it take you forever?"

He shrugged. "It's not going to be that tough. I created a bot that mines content from like a million different sites and then I'll probably use another bot to make sense of that information. It could be pretty cool. Even if we don't use it on our site I'll bet there'll be a lot we can use for the jobs we take on."

I had to admit that actually did sound super cool, and I just about told Marcus I thought so, but before I could sirens sounded in the distance and I groaned. "We need to be smarter next time," I muttered, "I don't want any of our jobs to actually hurt people."

Marcus nodded but didn't say anything. A fire truck rolled up a minute later. The firefighters jumped into action.

They pulled out hoses and stuff, but since there wasn't actually a fire two of them ran around to the side of the building, no doubt looking for the water shutoff valve. A couple of other firefighters went inside. A minute later they came out and gestured for Mr. Lee to come back into the store too.

"That was faster than we thought it'd be," I said. "A plumber would've taken a lot longer to get here. Do you think the water was even on long enough?"

"Dunno. It's not like I'm an expert on flowers. But I killed my mom's fern when I overwatered it. Must be the same for orchids and roses and daisies and whatever else he has in there."

I tried to sink even deeper into the shade. I kind of wished I'd been in the store when the sprinkler had come on just so I could cool down a bit.

Marcus wiped the sweat off his face with the bottom of his shirt. "Let's just see what happens."

As we watched, I thought about second request we got to take out Mr. Lee. It was the request that really put the florist into our crosshairs. It had been a genuine request from an adult. It was simple. It was direct. And it was from a woman named Deloris. She was newly married and claimed Mr. Lee ruined her wedding. She filled out our online form with three simple sentences that read:

This jerk ruined my wedding by bringing flowers to the reception that died before it started. He has no business being a florist. I will pay—gladly—to see him get what he deserves. —Deloris M.

She'd followed the instructions we posted and uploaded a photo as well as the street address for Mr. Lee's Flower Garden. Mr. Lee's small downtown shop had a sign announcing his store had a "focus on freshness." Yeah, right.

I'm not ashamed to admit that Marcus and I lost our minds a bit when the second request came in. Our reputation as professional fixers had made it to the ears of adults, and we couldn't wait to prove ourselves.

Our fire-sprinkler sabotage was the first part of our plan. There was a chance, we thought, that the sprinkler would be enough—that we'd have caused enough damage to shut the place down. It would serve as a message, an example of what we could do. Show everyone the Revengers weren't do-gooders. We were ruthless. Sure we only took jobs we believed in—jobs taking down people we believed deserved to be taken down—but we wanted our reputation to speak for itself. And we wanted clients to know one thing: once we accepted a job, we were in it to win it.

Turned out, though, that the first part of our plan wasn't enough. Not even close.

Fifteen minutes after the alarm went off, the firefighters were already packing up their gear. I nudged Marcus. We walked casually across the street and toward the strip mall and joined the onlookers who were being held back by the firefighters. We slipped between people and slowly made our way through the crowd to where a yellow-tape perimeter flapped. Mr. Lee stood talking to one of the firefighters.

"A faulty sprinkler head?" Mr. Lee waved a hand out. "I didn't even know those things could be faulty."

The firefighter removed his helmet and rubbed the back of his neck. His fire jacket hung open, unzipped, and he looked like he wanted to go back into the flower shop and start that sprinkler again to cool off.

"Oh, sure. I've seen it before. I suggest having all the sprinkles checked by professionals. If they're not installed right they can go off during heat waves like we've been having this past week." The firefighter looked at the building and shook his head. "To tell you the truth, what happened in there is almost one of those happy accidents, what do they call that? There's a word for it I think...?"

"Serendipity," Mr. Lee grumbled.

"Yeah, that's it. I mean, you have a store that's essentially built to handle water spills—large drains, tiled floors, rubber baseboards. The only sprinkler that went off was in the middle of the store, right over the bulk of your stock. I'm no gardener, but I bet your flowers have been feeling the effects of the city's water restrictions. They'll probably be better off thanks to your inside rain."

Mr. Lee's shoulders slumped and he glared at his own shop. "Yeah, I guess you're right."

Serendipity wasn't a word I'd known before, but we weren't trying to give Mr. Lee any happy accidents.

I nudged Marcus and we backed into the crowd and headed back down the street.

In the end, it was the third request that really sealed the deal with our decision to take out Mr. Lee. It just made our target too interesting to pass up. We were already formulating a plan to take the guy down because we were sure Angry Bride would pay up if we really got the guy. But when we received the third request, well, the stakes rose to a whole other level. That request was from someone who wanted the shop closed down once and for all and it came from someone we'd never have expected—Mr. Lee himself. The guy actually wanted himself to be taken out, and he'd called on the Revengers to do it.

We didn't know why he wanted to be a target, but we also didn't care. We were just happy to oblige.

CHAPTER TWO

Our sprinkler sabotage was a massive failure. Not only had it *not* destroyed the stock, or the store, the firefighter had basically said our intervention actually made it possible for the florist to get around the water restrictions the city was dishing out. His flowers were probably going to be the best in town.

I decided before the trucks rolled away from the scene that we'd leave that part out when we posted the job-details on our website. I also felt badly about tying up the fire department for a prank.

We shook off the bust and launched immediately into the next phase of our plan—that included learning everything we could about the target, and it was an excellent opportunity to test our stalking skills—which Marcus swore was a fundamental skill for Revengers to have and would give us the edge when we ever saved enough money for the spy camp.

Tall and thin, Mr. Lee reminded me of a metal fence pole. That made following him pretty easy. Marcus and I decided pretty early on that one of the Revenger policies would be to learn as much as possible about our targets. We planned on having

files on everyone, background information that we could use to make our plans. But so far our file on Mr. Lee was paper-thin. He was single, lived alone, and worked as a florist. That was about it. We weren't sure how old he was, but we figured he had to be a few years older than my dad. Marcus bet he was in his forties or maybe really early fifties. I thought that sounded right.

"We should actually call her Angry Bride," Marcus said.

"What are you talking about?" I asked, keeping my focus on our target. Mr. Lee had closed his shop about the same time the fire trucks left, and had begun walking down the street. We'd been following him for a while. He'd gone home — which was a small house not far from his shop — and changed out of his wet clothes. He stopped at a drugstore and bought a pack of mints. Since then his pace had doubled, at first we thought he'd spotted us and was trying to get away, but then decided he must've been running late for something.

I was tired and sweaty and I couldn't decide if the heat or Marcus's stupid comments bothered me more.

Marcus swiped at the sweat on his forehead. "I mean, Angry Bride can be the code name for Deloris. Plus, it sounds like we're saying Angry Bird, so even if someone does hear us, they'll think we're talking about that old game you used to play."

I blinked. "Um... you played it too, and I think you're overthinking this. No one is listening to us, and if we said Deloris or Angry Bride, or Deloris the Angry Bride, it wouldn't matter because, again, no one is listening to us. But if you're worried about it, maybe just keep your mouth shut when we're around other people."

"Oh, people are listening, Jared." He made a scene of turning his head left then right. He dropped his voice to a whisper. "People are always listening."

"Give me a break."

"We need code names," he said in his normal voice. "And they should be cool like—" Suddenly, he grabbed my arm and pulled me off the sidewalk and behind a tree. I thought he was still playing up the drama of his code-name idea so I smacked his hand away. But he gestured up ahead and it didn't look like he was kidding, so I turned.

Mr. Lee had stopped on the street corner. My mind went to the recreation center that wasn't far from where we were, and the park with shade-giving trees, or better yet the giant indoor pool filled with cool water. I crossed my fingers and hoped Mr. Lee was headed there. He checked his phone and started walking again, his pace even faster than before.

"Who do you think he's meeting?" Marcus asked as we started after him again.

I shrugged. "I don't care as long as we figure out a good way to take him out. I know our sprinkler plan was supposed to be phase one, but we hadn't meant to make his business better. Besides, if the man *wants* to be targets of the Revengers, the least we could do is make it quick."

Sweat dripped down my back. We rounded the corner just in time to see him duck into the rec center.

"Hurry," I said, feeling a sudden rush of excitement. "Air-conditioning awaits."

We burst through the doors and into a blast of cold air.

Marcus shivered and I closed my eyes for a second as the cool relief washed over me. When I opened them I saw Mr. Lee at the far end of the lobby, heading toward the stairs that led to the second floor. I knew the building well, and the second level had a big deck that overlooked the pool and a large food-court style cafeteria. Mr. Lee towered over the other people. From the way folks were hanging out it seemed like most everyone had come here just to escape the heat. We didn't need to be so worried about being seen now—there were loads of kids our age wandering around. We followed Mr. Lee up the stairs and realized all at once why he'd come.

The restaurants on the second floor were situated against the back wall, with tables and chairs filling the rest of the space all the way to a curved glass wall that looked out over the indoor pool. Today, however, a large section of the room—nearly half—had been sectioned off with rope. Every table in that section had a woman sitting alone with a pencil and what looked like a score card—like the kind you'd use on a mini-golf course.

"Speed dating," Marcus said, pointing to a large sign that said just that. The sign had an image of a clock inside a heart and said, *Matched in a Minute.*

Mr. Lee stepped up to a table near an opening to the roped section. He said something to the man at the table and then picked up a sticker name badge and pressed it to his chest. Then he joined the dozen or so other men waiting.

Some of the guys shifted their weight nervously; others glanced around like they were worried someone would see them. A few looked normal—like Mr. Lee—but most of the men leered at the women like hungry animals.

"Is this ... voluntary?" I asked.

Marcus pointed across the room to a table on the non-dating side. It stood close enough to the roped-off area that we'd be able to hear some of what was being said at a few of the dating tables.

I grabbed a seat and Marcus grabbed some fries and two Cokes from one of the food counters. When he came back a bell rang and guys started heading out to various tables. At the table closest to us sat a serious-looking woman.

She looked like a librarian from the movies—hair pulled back, glasses over her small eyes, sour mouth pulled down, and a stuffy all-business kind of coat and skirt and buttoned-up shirt. When the conversation began it was clear she intended to use her sixty seconds to the fullest. The way she grilled the guys that landed at her table you'd have thought she was interrogating them for suspected criminal activity. I felt a bit sorry for the guys, but grateful we'd managed to get close enough to hear the conversations.

The bell rang again and all the guys swapped seats. Mr. Lee took a seat a couple tables away from Ms. Librarian. It wouldn't be long before we'd hear how he fared against the woman.

"What do you do?" Ms. Librarian asked.

The guy who'd just come over to her table hadn't even had a chance to sit down. "Oh, um, I, um, I work in finance. What about you?"

"HR. Kids?"

"Um, none yet." The poor guy glanced at his watch and looked around like maybe sixty seconds was going to be too long a time with Ms. HR-Librarian.

She gave him a tired look. "So then you do want some?"

"Why? Are you looking to sell a few?" He laughed and seemed to see she hadn't even cracked a smile.

"Man," Marcus whispered. "This is painful."

The questions went on like that—rapid fire—until the bell rang again. All the guys stood and shuffled to the next table. There were two more rounds before Mr. Lee landed at Ms. HR-Librarian's table.

"I'm Andrew," he said and put out his hand to shake hers.

She stared at his hand like he'd offered her a snake. "What do you do, Andrew?" She didn't say her own name.

Mr. Lee smiled. "I have a flower shop. What about you?"

"HR," she said, the words clipped. She narrowed her eyes even more and pushed her glasses up on her nose. "You don't look like a florist."

Mr. Lee shifted in his chair and asked, "What does a florist look like?"

I was surprised how calm he sounded and how confident he looked. Ms. HR-Librarian reminded me too much of Mr. Shevchenko, a substitute teacher we'd had at school who could terrify anyone in any class. I wouldn't want to be sitting with her.

She shrugged. "Have you always wanted to be a florist?"

Mr. Lee shook his head. "Have you always wanted to be in HR?"

"It seemed the obvious choice." She tapped the tip of her pen on the table. "I'm a people person."

Marcus choked on a fry and started coughing like he was dying. I thumped him on the back and tried to block him from everyone's stare. A second later, Marcus got it under control.

"I inherited the place," Mr. Lee said. "It was my dad's, and he passed a few years ago and I just sort of landed in it. I'm not quite as drawn to the business as he was."

"So you're, what? Honor bound to run the place? You don't have a choice."

"Something like that."

"And if you weren't? What would you do then?"

Mr. Lee smiled. "There was a time I thought I'd make a decent travel writer." He glanced up at the ceiling as if seeing something other than white tiles and air ducts. "I loved to imagine visiting all kinds of exotic locations." Sitting up, he looked hopeful for a moment and asked, "Have you done any traveling?"

"Outside of the country?" Her mouth tightened and she tapped her pen again. "No, thank you. That's never interested me. If it's what you want to do, why aren't you doing it?"

"I suppose I'd need a reason to leave the shop. An excuse to close the family business I run with my brother and his son."

"Such as love?" the woman asked.

Mr. Lee shrugged. "More like a fire." He opened his mouth to ask another question, but the bell rang.

The woman kept her head down over her score card. Mr. Lee gave her a nod and shuffled to the next table. I looked at Marcus as the next unlucky soul took a seat across from the woman with no name.

Marcus smiled and shoved a fry in his mouth. "At least we know why he wants out. And what's more, he's given us a great idea for how to do it."

"What? You mean a fire?" I shook my head. "He was joking."

"Was he?"

After draining my Coke, I rattled the ice in the drink cup. "We just finished trying to kill all his stock with water. We're not going to turn around and burn his place down."

Marcus's mouth curved up in an evil grin. "Aren't we?"

CHAPTER THREE

After we'd stepped out of the rec center and back into a wall of heat—a guy can only take so much speed dating—Marcus turned to me.

"Okay, I agree we shouldn't burn his store down. But Mr. Lee wants out. That's the key. That's how we take him out, we destroy his shop somehow. Angry Bride gets what she wants, the people of this city get a bad flower guy gone, and he gets what he wants."

"I thought you were against missions where everyone ended up happy? And would you please stop calling her Angry Bride?"

"That's her code name." He grinned. "And I'm not against someone getting what they want as long as it works with what we want too. I just don't want jerks to leave happy. And I don't think this guy is a jerk anymore. A bit of a weirdo, totally. Not the best florist, sure. But not a jerk. I mean, you heard him—he inherited the place. He feels like he has to keep it."

We spent the walk home working out possible ways to destroy the man's business without destroying the man—or committing illegal acts of arson. We thought of some great ones too. Buying a crate of termites and releasing them into his walls.

But it wasn't easy to find a place where you could buy termites by the crate and besides, they'd take forever. We thought about throwing some rats into his shop and calling the health department.

But it was a flower shop, not a restaurant. We scratched that idea when we decided that was nothing a few traps wouldn't solve, anyway. In the end, Marcus came up with the best plan. But he didn't think of it until after we made it back to his house and our brains were half melted from the heat.

Sitting in Marcus's room, eating ice cream and surfing the net on Marcus's tablet, Marcus said, "What if we just made it so Mr. Lee was forced to take a break from flowers? I mean, it's risky. He might just come back and start again, but what if we force him to close his shop for a few weeks? We could give him the chance to have an adventure and if that sparks him into being a travel writer he'll just sell his business." He looked at me with a huge smile. "What do you think?"

"I think I don't even know your plan and you're smiling like a fat kid who just found a cookie. C'mon already. Spill."

"We steal all his flowers," Marcus said. He held up his hand as if he wanted a high five for coming up with the idea. I groaned, and he quickly added, "I mean, we buy out his stock, and then he's got nothing to do until he an restock."

"Yeah," I said, "Because he probably gets his flowers from, like, Uzbekistan and that will take like a month." I shook my head. "And buying all the flowers would be good for his business, not bad for it." I saw Marcus about to speak and I threw up my hands. "We're not going to try to flood his store again either." Marcus deflated slightly, and I added, "We need to be smarter. We need to think outside the box on this one."

Marcus shifted on his chair. He stirred his ice cream. He liked it best when it was melted. "Okay. What if we just kill all his plants with weed killer?" When I didn't say anything he added, "You hate it, don't you?"

"I don't hate it, Marcus. It's just, well, whatever can kill plants might kill a person too. And what do we know about poisoning anything. Look, we have three people who might pay us for this job, so we have to be smart about it. We have to actually give each of them what they want, and that includes Mr. Lee. I doubt very much he'd pay up if we accidently put him in the hospital. What we need is a way for us to look ruthless to the whiny kids and angry bride, but also, we need Mr. Lee to experience something that puts him back on track to being a travel writer. He needs to decide to leave the flower shop on his own—or at least think the decision is his own."

"What do you suggest," Marcus asked. "Start a travel blog for him? Fake a contest and buy him a trip to that Uzbekistan place you mentioned?"

"Those aren't the worst ideas in the world," I said.

"Yes," Marcus said. "They are. They're truly awful. We need a win like we had with Shevchenko."

Shevchenko, or Mr. Shev as we used to call him, had been one of our first jobs. We'd gotten rid of him by making it look like he was a wanted criminal from Ukraine and he was deported. It was some of our finest work.

It worked out well for him in the end since he got a crazy settlement out of his false arrest and deportation, but we didn't advertise that.

Marcus must've read something in my face because he added, "Okay, so we didn't *really* destroy Shevchenko, but he's not teaching anymore is he? So point goes to us. We're getting really good at this. And I still think we're on the right track with the key being to reignite Mr. Lee's inner adventurer. He seemed really excited when he talked about being a travel writer."

I put down my empty bowl and stood up. "Okay. Let's take the evening. After dinner we re-group and come up with an idea. I'll call you. We'll think of something awesome."

"We'd better—or we may just have to stop calling ourselves Revengers and start calling ourselves the Dream Makers." He shivered. "I don't want to be a dream maker, Jared."

I didn't want to be one either and I left Marcus determined not to let that happen.

CHAPTER FOUR

My dad's car was in the driveway when I walked up. The trunk was open and as I got closer I realized there were two small suitcases inside.

"Mom?" I called as I stepped through the door. My sister Ronie came careening around a corner and we nearly smashed into each other. At the last second she pivoted and spun like quarterback. She dumped her duffle bag at the door.

"You're in trouble," she said, almost singing the words. She flashed a snarky grin that said she knew something I didn't. She saw the flower in my hand I'd picked up outside Mr. Lee's and frowned. "That's not going to save you." She turned and bounded up the stairs two at a time to her room.

"Trouble," I said to myself. I tried to think of something I'd done that my folks wouldn't like. The only thing I could come up with was that they knew about the Revengers. A lump stuck in my throat and I couldn't swallow around it. I knew Marcus wouldn't say anything about our business, but I hoped he hadn't been lazy about making sure the Internet fingerprint didn't lead back to either of us.

"Where have you been?" Mom practically yelled.

I jumped and looked up to see her standing in front of me. "W-with Marcus. Why?"

She marched past me and called up the stairs, "Ronie, don't forget your jacket, dear. We'll likely go out tonight and it'll be cool." She turned back to me. "You're late." I must have given her a confused look because she said, "Remember, I told you I needed you home today to watch Sky until the sitter gets here."

My eyes widened. "I totally thought you were kidding."

"Jared!" She let out a long breath. "You knew we were going away for the night for Ronie's meet."

My sister had a gymnastics competition. I knew that. Since she'd gotten some fancy former-Olympian-Russian coach she'd been killing it at competitions. That hadn't been the part I'd thought she'd been joking about. "I meant the babysitter. I thought you were joking about getting a sitter. I'm eleven, Mom. I think I can take care of myself for one night."

"And Sky?"

"Take her with you. She likes girl stuff. I'll be fine on my own."

Mom frowned at me. "We're not riding ponies and braiding hair, Jared. This is a big competition for your sister. It wouldn't be fun for Sky. Be here for your sister, okay?"

"Mom!" Ronie yelled, "Did you pack my shoes?"

"Yes, dear. They're already in the car." Mom slipped on her shoes and gave me a hug. "Your Aunt Rebecca will be here in a few minutes to babysit. She called to say she was on her way, just running a couple minutes late. But we have to get going if we're going to beat traffic out of the city."

Aunt Rebecca? I groaned. "Oh, c'mon! She's not even our real aunt." And she wasn't. She was just a close friend of my mom's who had always been called Aunt Rebecca. I hadn't learned the truth until I was eight. I'd felt totally cheated. I mean, who makes you call someone "aunt" who isn't your aunt? It wasn't right. But as soon as I found out she wasn't my real aunt I stopped feeling guilty about not liking her. Here's the thing about Aunt Rebecca: if there was a competition for being over-protective and safety-conscious, she'd win it at the Olympics. *Cautious* wasn't a strong enough word to describe her.

I thought of one more way to get out of this and went for it. "Can we at least get a different sitter? Someone who doesn't believe dust-mites are going to attack us in our sleep, maybe also someone who didn't grow up during the last ice age?"

My mom gasped. "Ice age? We're the same age, I'll have you know."

Dad stepped into the foyer, smiling. "Ah, the ice age. It feels like just yesterday." He put his hand on my shoulder. "Did I ever tell you how I met your mom? It was the day of the great glacier melt and all the cave people came out for it. And there she was—"

Mom smacked his shoulder, smiling. "Don't you encourage him."

I held out my hands. "I only meant it would be nice if we could just have a normal babysitter sometimes. Or better yet, *no* babysitter."

"Sky loves her," my mom said. "And we trust her. She'll keep you both safe."

I turned to my dad, but he looked away, trying not to laugh. I knew what he was thinking because I was thinking the same thing. "Safe, Mom? Are you kidding? She's so safe she's actually un-safe. She once said the living room rug was dangerous because we could trip on the edge so she rolled it up and then Sky slipped on the hardwood floor. She nearly broke her neck!"

Mom cupped my chin and looked at me, her eyes soft and her mouth curving up a little. Her mind was made up. I wasn't going to change anything. "Be nice to her, Jared. She's like family to me. She should be like family to you."

Sky slipped around Mom and stuck herself to my side. She tucked her hand into mine and looked up at me with her huge green eyes. Her brown curls stuck up around her head. "I love Aunt Rebecca. She smells like cinnamon." Sky's voice practically dripped with sugar, like only a kid's voice her age could. I didn't have a chance.

"You know what else smells like cinnamon?" I muttered. "Zombies."

Sky gasped. "Aunt Rebecca's a zombie?"

My dad leveled a glare my direction and told Sky, "Your brother is just being silly. And you're right, Sky. Aunt Rebecca is perfectly lovable." He turned to me. "Jared, I expect you to help Rebecca with Sky. It's been a while since she babysat you guys."

"Hasn't been long enough," I muttered quiet enough that I didn't think anyone heard.

"It's just one night," Dad said. "Show us you can be grown up about this and maybe next time we need to go out we'll talk about letting you stay home alone." My mom cleared her throat. Dad glanced at her and looked back at me again. "We'll *talk* about it, understand?"

I decided to make one last attempt at avoiding my fake aunt. "Does it have to be Aunt Rebecca?" I said. "What if we used that sitter down the street—Rylee what's her name?" I knew exactly who Rylee was—Rylee Hottie Matthews. At sixteen she was the assistant captain of the cheerleading team at Sutter High School. I'd have done just about anything to get my folks to hire her as the babysitter any night of the week.

Ronie came running down the stairs. She stopped next to me, bouncing on her toes, and rubbed my head. "Awe, you have a crush on Rylee Martin, huh, little man? How cute."

I smacked her hand away. "I don't have a crush. It was just a suggestion."

Ronie grinned. You wouldn't look at Ronie and see a gymnast. She'd dyed her hair almost black and she had on baggy jeans and one of Dad's t-shirts. But she was actually really good. And when she competed she was out to win. I didn't like a lot about my sister, but I liked that she took out her competition like a Revenger. And also, that she never bragged about it. Not ever. She didn't even keep any of her trophies in her room. She'd said something about them not being cool once. But Mom kept them all in the garage—and there were boxes and boxes of them.

"At least you'll be *safe* with Aunt Rebecca," Ronie said, just quiet enough so I could hear her but my parents wouldn't.

I clenched my back teeth and let out a scream in my head. Mom must have seen something on my face. She put a hand on my shoulder and said, "Oh, c'mon, Jared. She's not so bad."

"Mom, last time she watched me brush my teeth and freaked out when I used more than a pea-sized amount of toothpaste. She actually called poison control!"

My dad laughed. "These will be great stories one day. You really should write them down."

My mom kissed my head. "So she's a bit cautious. Remember, she worked for an insurance company for years. She's just a bit more *aware* of how dangerous the world can be."

I knew the story, of course. I'd been reminded of my aunt's past every time she'd come to babysit. She used to work as an insurance adjuster and she'd gone to all these crazy accidents and wrote reports on how they could have been avoided. According to my mom, all the disasters got to her. She'd apparently developed some kind of post-traumatic stress and started seeing danger everywhere. I felt bad for her, but I didn't understand why I had to put up with her brand of crazy. Especially when there was a perfectly hot babysitter down the street.

"You'll be fine," Mom said. "We'll be back tomorrow evening about this time."

She bent down to hug and kiss Sky, and I thought about not being in the house tomorrow. If I could get out early enough, I might not even have to see Aunt Rebecca the whole day.

"Have fun, you two," Mom said. She hugged and kissed us both a second time, and then my dad hugged and kissed Sky. He reached out to do the same to me. I held up my hand and shook my head. I was a Revenger—Revengers weren't huggers.

Mom called back as she headed toward the car, "Jared, look after your sister, okay? Your aunt just texted—she's only a few minutes away."

I nodded and muttered, "Not my aunt."

After they drove off, I slumped against the doorway, wondering what I was going to do. Aunt Rebecca's post-traumatic paranoia about safety meant that she was hyper aware of everything. She'd know if I was sneaking around. She'd probably bring helmets and kneepads and force us to wear them just to walk around the house. In fact, if Sky had any money at all, I'd have bet her we'd both be wearing bubble-wrap jackets before the end of the day.

I grabbed the phone off the counter and punched in Marcus's number.

"Hey, it's me," I said.

"Hey, man, I was just working on that new website. I feel way better now that we're out of that heat. When are you coming over? I've got a few ideas about that other thing we're working on."

That other thing? Obviously one of his parents were nearby. "Yeah, about that. I'm not a hundred percent sure I'll be able to get over to your place tonight." I glanced down at Sky who was galloping a plastic pony over the wall beside me.

"Why?" Marcus asked.

I wasn't sure what to say. I knew what would happen if I told him my parents had hired a sitter for me and Sky. I groaned and decided to just do it like I was pulling off a Band-Aid. "My parents just took off, and—"

"Perfect!" Marcus said, not letting me finish. "My parents are going out to dinner tonight too. It'll give us time to lock down this florist thing."

"Marcus, I need you to focus and listen to me. It's going to be tougher to meet up because..." I let the words fade into a sigh.

"Why? Spit it out already."

"My folks hired a babysitter," I blurted. "I have to wait until she gets here and I may have to stay to help look after Sky."

A long pause came over the phone line. Like I'd thought, Marcus started to laugh.

"Thanks, man," I told him. "That makes me feel so much better."

He stopped laughing abruptly. "Wait, is it that the hot babysitter who lives on your block?"

"Do you think I'd be complaining if it was Rylee?" I asked.

"Guess not." He started laughing again. When he had it almost under control he choked out, "That's so funny, man. I haven't had a sitter since I was, like, three or something."

"Yeah, yeah. I know. My parents said she's not here for me. She'll be looking after Sky."

"Riiiight." Marcus gave another laugh. I couldn't blame him. I would have been laughing at him if he'd been the one stuck with a sitter. "Okay. If we can't get together tonight we should meet up early tomorrow."

"Sounds good," I said. "See you then."

After I hung up I lowered my head to the countertop. Some Revenger I was, left with a babysitter.

Sky tugged on my jeans and whispered, "Jared?" She swiped a lock of brown hair out of her eyes and said, "Is Aunt Rebecca really a zombie?"

"Do you even know what a zombie is?" I asked.

She put her hands on her hips. "Of course I do. Dead people who come back to life and eat brains."

I considered going for it and making Sky think Aunt Rebecca was a zombie. But Sky was only six, and I couldn't bring myself to freak her out like that. Maybe that would have been funny if she didn't still believe in the Tooth Fairy or Santa Claus. Instead, I shook my head. "I was kidding, Sky. Aunt Rebecca is not a zombie. She's just a lady who smells like cinnamon."

A sharp knock shook the front door.

One night, I told myself as Sky and I headed to the front door. *I can handle one night.*

When I opened the door, there was Aunt Rebecca, looking slightly disheveled and anxious. A roll of bubble wrap poked out from under one arm and she hefted a duffle bag in the other hand.

Bubble wrap? I'd only been kidding to think of that but it didn't look like she was kidding at all.

CHAPTER FIVE

Aunt Rebecca looked like a nurse at the end of a double-shift. But that was pretty much how she always looked. My mom said it was because she worked too hard, and my dad said it was because worrying all the time has worn her out. But it could've also been because she didn't wear makeup—she'd said something once about how you could put your eye out with those little makeup wand thingies.

She had on a dress, and her dark hair was pulled back into a lose pony-tail. Her eyes, as she stared at me from the doorway, gave a familiar *worried* stare.

"Hello, Jared," she said with a weak, but sincere smile. She crouched as Sky ran up and hugged her. "Hi, Sky, I'm sorry for being late. Something didn't feel right about my car and I had to get it checked out."

I didn't say a thing. She could've been a hundred hours late and I wouldn't have asked where she'd been. The last thing I wanted was to listen to her launch into one of her safety lectures.

"Well," she said with a friendly grin, "at least I'm here now." She set her bags down and looked around the room. "What do you say we make this place just a bit safer?"

I eyed the bubble wrap. I could already picture her nailing it up over the walls and all the furniture too.

"Won't take long. Just won't feel comfortable if we don't dull some of these sharp edged I know you guys have around here." She turned her attention to the room and scanned from left to right. When she was done she shivered and handed Sky the roll of bubble wrap. My sister squealed with excitement. Aunt Rebecca dug into her duffle bag and pulled out a large plastic container filled with pieces of plastic.

"Electrical outlet covers," she said and gave me a wink. "Would you mind being a dear and putting one into each plug you can find that aren't in use?"

"Um, Aunt Rebecca, Sky and I know better than to shove things into power outlets. We know what would happen." I turned to my sister. "Right, Sky?"

Sky nodded and acted like she'd gotten a bad electric shock by going stiff as a board and shaking.

"Oh, my goodness!" Aunt Rebecca screamed. "Call nine-one-one."

"She's just pretending!" I said.

Aunt Rebecca dropped to her knees beside Sky. My sister was already laughing again. Aunt Rebecca blew out a breath. "You are an excellent actor, Sky." She forced a smile and added, "I thought you were having a seizure. Please, for the sake of my heart, no more pretending."

Sky giggled and asked, "What's a seizure?"

I took my tub of outlet covers and walked away while Aunt Rebecca began explaining medical stuff Sky would never understand. By the time I'd blocked every outlet I could find, Sky and Aunt Rebecca were laughing in the living room. Good. That meant I didn't have to stick around.

"All done, Aunt Rebecca. Every plug is now safe from fingers and forks and bits from my collection of metal scraps." Aunt Rebecca's eyes widened. "I'm kidding," I said making a mental note not to joke with my Aunt again. "I gestured for the door. "I'm heading to my friend's house for dinner, but I'll be back later. I put his number on the fridge."

"Are you sure you can get there okay? It's not too dark?"

I glanced at the window. It wasn't even five o'clock and the sun was still in the sky. It might as well have been noon. "I think I'll manage," I said.

Aunt Rebecca bit her lip. "I suppose your mom did say you could have some freedom while they were gone. But I don't want you walking back when it's dark. Call me for a ride, or have your friend's parents drive you home, okay?"

I almost said that Marcus's parents were out for the night, but I bit off the words. Who knew what she'd do if she heard we'd be unsupervised? "He lives about four blocks from here. I won't need a ride. Besides, I've got my bike." She had that worried expression on again so I added, "Also, bonus, I'll be getting some good-for-my-health exercise, so that'll be a good thing, right?"

"Do you know how many people are hit by cars while walking or riding their bikes?"

I held back a groan. "Not of the top of my head. But I imagine—"

"Millions!" She waved a hand at me like I was about to be one of those millions.

"Really?" I somehow doubted that but decided not to say so. "Thank you for, um, making me, uh, *aware*. And yes, I'll call when I get there."

She stepped between me and the front door. "And when you leave."

I slipped on my shoes. I would have said anything to get out of there. "Of course. I'll call before I leave there too."

I reached for the door knob.

"Where's your helmet?"

"Strapped to my bike. And, yes, don't worry, I'll wear it." I glanced at my sister who'd gone back to galloping her plastic pony. "Have fun, Sky."

I'd only made it a few steps across the porch before I heard, "Oh, wait!"

Letting out a breath, I turned back. Aunt Rebecca stepped out onto the porch. She had something in her hands. I glanced at it, but before could react she'd swiped her hands across my back and chest. I glanced down. She'd slapped a cross of reflective tape over my shirt.

I blinked. "Awesome. Thank you." Then I muttered, "Now I can get that part-time job as a Crossing Guard I've been hoping to get."

Aunt Rebecca's expression softened and she smiled. "I'm being overprotective, aren't I?" She didn't wait for me to answer before adding, "It's only because I care, and I know the world in...sort of a different way than most other people do."

I paused and resisted the urge to tear the tape off my clothes and bolt for the door before Aunt Rebecca decided I needed to become even more reflective. "It's okay, Aunt Rebecca, I get it." I took a step back towards the door. "I know you care, and I'm glad my mom left you in charge of Sky." I touched the reflective tape on my clothes and forced myself to smile as I backed away even more. "Thanks for this. I settled on getting out of there and left the strips of reflective tape on my shirt. I forced a smile and said, "Thanks so much." Then I pivoted and ducked stepped outside into the sun.

Sky poked her head out of the door as I got on my bike. "See you in a couple hours, Sky."

Sky grinned and pointed at me. "You look like a crossing guard."

"Wonderful," I muttered. I threw on my helmet and hoped onto my bike before Aunt Rebecca could do or say anything else.

Marcus's house really was only a few blocks away and in less than five minutes I was knocking on his front door. At least I could have a moment of *normal* while I was hanging out with Marcus. His parents weren't at all over protective and were actually kind of the opposite. He'd been allowed to ride the subway on his own since he was ten, and his parents would even leave him home alone overnight when they'd go to work conferences. Marcus wasn't messed up from having that freedom. He was probably the most normal guy I knew.

I'd barely finished that thought when the door swung open and there stood my *normal* friend, wearing a ninja costume.

We stood there for a second, staring at each other. "Are you going to explain?" I asked.

"Explain what?" He gestured to my shirt. "And what's up with all the reflective tape? You going for a job at the crossing guard academy?"

"Very funny." I waved my hand at him. "Seriously, what is all of this?"

"Um, training. What does it look like?"

Usually we trained on the paintball course, but the heat had kept us away from anything that meant wearing more than t-shirts and shorts outdoors. The thought of wearing coveralls and running around in full sunlight made me cringe. Marcus ducked back inside his house. I followed him into the coolness of maximum air conditioning. Marcus had an obstacle course of cushions and furniture set up.

"Check it out." With a grin, he ran at an ottoman. He jumped and almost cleared the small piece of furniture. But his foot clipped the edge.

He hit the carpet with a heavy *thud.* Wheezing and gasping followed.

Leaning over him, I said, "You're a credit to ninjas around the globe. Now stop messing around and let's plan how we're going to get this florist taken out."

CHAPTER SIX

When Marcus finally caught his breath he got up and collapsed on the sofa.

"Okay," I said. "When we talked on the phone you said you had an idea. Let's hear it."

He sat up. "Right, well, I was thinking. You know how your mom's a drug dealer? Well—"

"Hold it!" I said, cutting him off. "She's not a drug dealer. She's a sales rep. She goes around telling doctors about new drugs and gives them free samples."

Marcus pointed at me. "There. The free sample drug thing. What did I say? Do you think she has anything strong enough to knock out Mr. Lee?" I stared at him, trying to decide if he was serious or if he'd hit his head too hard when he'd fallen over the ottoman. He must've thought I wanted him to explain it better, because he launched into his idea again. "Here's what I propose: we grind up some of your mom's really potent drugs, then take them to the flower shop. While you distract him with questions about the proper care of orchids or dandelions or something, I dust one of his roses with the powered up pills."

I opened my mouth to stop him from continuing but Marcus cut me off. "Wait, this is the best part. Next we tell him to hand us the rose with the drugs on it, he gets poked by one of the thorns and the drugs get into his blood, and Blmao!"

"Blamo?" I asked, wishing I hadn't.

"He drops like a sack of plant food. And we, you know..." He scratched the back of his neck. "Do something with him. Put him in a sack or something."

"A sack? Just put him in a sack?"

"We could use a box if you think that would be better."

"Do you even realize how dumb that sounds? Not only does it have like a zero chance of success, but you're also talking about drugging a guy and putting him in a sack."

"I said we could use a box."

"Do you even realize how illegal that would be? We'd be in prison for the rest of our lives. And for good reason since we'd be insane to do that."

Marcuse squinted at me. "So... no?"

"No." Folding my arms, I shook my head. "A thousand times no."

His phone rang in the kitchen. While Marcus went to answer it I sat down on a big overstuffed chair, put my hands behind my head, and blew out a breath. There had to be a reasonable way to take care of Mr. Lee. But then again, maybe it was one of those too-good-to-be-true jobs and it was making us consider too many risky moves. It might just be better to walk away from the Mr. Lee job. But then I caught a glimpse of Marcus's laptop screen. Call it fate, or luck, or who knows what, but my eyes were drawn to an ad in the top corner of the screen. An ad for exactly what we needed. Marcus had already found the perfect answer and didn't even seem to know it.

I was about to call out to Marcus when he stepped into the room, holding out his phone to me. "It's for you."

"Jared?" It was Aunt Rebecca's voice and there was an edge of panic to it.

I'd forgotten to call her when I arrived. But that was only a minute ago. "Hi, Aunt Rebecca. Sorry I for—"

"You said it took five minutes." Her voice sounded squeaky, higher than normal, and she rushed her words. "We were worried sick over here. I just about called the police."

What? Had she timed me? I turned to Marcus and tapped the top of his computer screen, telling him to look at what I'd found—we'll what he'd found, really. Trying to hang onto my cool, I said, "I'm sorry, Aunt Rebecca. I was just about to call you. I got here with no problem. From now on I'll be better about calling you."

She went on about how I'd nearly given her a heart attack. I had to promise I'd come back before it got dark just to get her off the phone.

When I hung up, Marcus was staring at me like he'd just watched a scene from a horror movie. "What in the world was that about?"

"Babysitter," I said, hoping that would be the end of it. It wasn't.

"I can almost see your house from here, you could probably stand up on my roof and wave to your aunt."

"Right," I said, "and search and rescue would be helicoptering into your back-yard thirty seconds after she saw me on your roof. I'm telling you, man, it's unreal." I gestured to his computer, hoping to change the subject. "What do you think?"

He blinked and turned back to his computer. "Oh, right. No, that looks absolutely brilliant. I can't even believe something like this exists. It's so incredible!"

Marcus clicked on an ad and a website came up called *Adventure Plus Enterprises*. They had a list of adventures you could buy, and not just the usual travel to faraway places type of adventures. It had a bunch that were for people looking for adventures that went beyond the expectations. There were packages like *The Underground* which apparently took people on secret underground adventure through tunnels beneath the city. Or *The Escape,* where participants are locked in a room and have to follow hidden clues to escape. Or the *Epic Survival* package where they'd take you and drop you off in some crazy remote location and you had to make your own way back to civilization.

It was actually super cool idea and there were loads of packages Marcus and I would've loved to try. We spent close to an hour just exploring the options and taking about them, until we eventually settled on the perfect one for Mr. Lee.

"So this one then?" Marcus asked. "You're sure?"

I nodded.

He rubbed his hands together. "Oh, man, I was hoping you'd say that."

The plan was to give Mr. Lee way more than an adventure. He needed a jolt to his routine to figure out that the world was out there and he shouldn't waste time being unhappy. I really wanted to make that happen in the best Revenger-like way possible. And here was this company offering exactly what we needed. More than anything, we wanted him to disappear. That's what we said we'd do for Angry Bride. The street cred for Revengers was on the line.

"The K & R package," Marcus said, reading the site. "Kidnapping and ransom." He laughed as he read the description again. "Are you looking for some excitement but think skydiving and bungee jumping is for wimps? Then look no further, the K & R package with Adventure Plus Enterprises is guaranteed to get your blood pumping."

I had to admit, it sounded perfect, and the street cred we'd get from pulling this off would be insane. Of course, it wasn't until we'd settled on the plan that we looked at the price.

"A thousand dollars?" I said. "You're kidding me."

Marcus blew out a breath. He tapped his screen and brought up our account information for Revengers. We had just over eight hundred dollars left, but Marcus said he had a couple hundred dollars in Digi-coins in another account that he could use to pay the difference.

"But there's only one reason I'm willing to use my own money for this," he said. He brought up the APE site again and tapped the screen where bold letters spelled out a special offer:

BUY TODAY AND TAKE ADVANTAGE OF OUR TWO FOR ONE DEAL.

"Do you have someone in mind?" I asked.

"Well, duh." Marcus stood, tugged down his ninja outfit top, and pressed his hand to his chest. "Me."

"You?"

Marcus grinned. "Do you know how unbelievably cool it would be to experience that?"

"Being kidnapped?" I asked. "You really want to be grabbed off the street and tied up and stuffed somewhere dark and cold? Well... okay, maybe the cold isn't so bad right now."

"Oh, come on. A fake snatch and grab! To see how you'd deal with it?" He blew out a breath and kept grinning. "I seriously can't wait." I opened my mouth to tell him he was nuts, but he held up his hand. "I know what you're going to say. But listen, if I go with Mr. Lee, I can make sure he has the brainstorm we need him to have. I can totally use some Jedi mind tricks to influence him."

I thought about telling Marcus he wasn't a Jedi, but I remembered we didn't have enough money in the account to pull this off without his extra coins. And if he wanted to go along, who was I to stop him? Plus, it wasn't as though he'd be in any real danger.

"Fine," I said.

"Fine?" Marcus blinked. "Really?"

I slapped him on the shoulder. "Let's hire us some kidnappers."

CHAPTER SEVEN

*A*unt Rebecca called Marcus's house two more times. The first was to remind me that it was getting dark—even though it wasn't—and the second time was less than ten minutes later. Thanks to caller ID we decided not to answer that one, but I think she wanted to tell me the sky had started to look like setting-sun pink. As if changing sky colors, or a setting sun have been shown to cause instant death in twelve year olds.

"Your aunt is really... cautious, man," Marcus said.

"She's not my aunt."

Marcus started to say something—probably to ask about that—but he shut his mouth and turned back to his computer.

His parents weren't going to be home until after ten. I'd hoped we could do more with the plan, but Aunt Rebecca was going to keep calling. I grabbed my stuff and headed for the door.

"I better get back. Sky has probably been in a bubble-wrap-cocoon for the past hour. I better go help the poor kid out."

Marcus laughed and walked me to the door. "I'll email you when I get a confirmation from the APE people about the plan. I can't wait to find out how things work. I mean, do you think they'll actually bust into my house and take me?"

"Your mom would have a heart attack."

"Good point. They've probably worked all the kinks out of it. I might have to say I'm staying with you that day." His eyes widened. "Or do you think it's going to be a few days? I mean, for a thousand dollars you'd think we'd get a few days, right?"

I shook my head. "I'm glad you're looking forward to having your face on a milk carton." I opened the door and nearly collapsed when I saw Aunt Rebecca standing on the porch, poised to knock on the door. Poor Sky, clutched in the woman's other hand.

"There you are!" Aunt Rebecca said, her eyes wide. "We were worried sick."

Sky bounced up and down. "Hi, Jared." She saw Marcus and started laughing hysterically. "Funny pajamas."

When she caught a glimpse of Marcus, Aunt Rebecca took a step back. Her hand came up in a sort-of defensive move, like she was ready to defend me and Sky against an attack from Marcus.

Marcus put his arms out to the side. "Have you guys really never seen a ninja in training?"

Sky giggled. I faced off with Aunt Rebecca. "We just talked like two minutes ago! I told you I was just about to leave."

Mouth pulling down, Aunt Rebecca glanced at her wristwatch. "That was... twelve minutes ago. You said it took five minutes to bike to your friend's house, which means you should have been home seven minutes ago. I thought you'd been hit by a truck and left in a ditch or something. Or that something had happened to you here." She peered into the house and seemed to take in all the technology in Marcus's house. "Electronics are a major cause of house fires."

I blew out a breath. *Just one day*, I told myself. I could do this for just one day. She was a friend of my mom's and I needed to keep Mom happy so next time she and Dad would just leave me home by myself. "You're right, Aunt Rebecca. Sorry I worried you." I had to really struggle to sound like I meant it but I thought I pulled it off. I pointed at Marcus. "He was just showing me some ninja moves."

Sky tugged her hand out of Aunt Rebecca's grip and clapped. "I want to see!"

Marcus didn't even hesitate. He rushed at the same ottoman he'd tried to jump over before, did exactly the same thing again, catching his toes on the tip as he tried to leap over. He landed in a heap on the floor. Aunt Rebecca clutched the front of her shirt with a gasp. Sky laughed. Before Aunt Rebecca could race across the room to check on Marcus, which I'm sure she was gearing up to do, Marcus jumped up and did a ring master's bow, as if his crash had been planned from the start.

Aunt Rebecca stabbed a shaking finger at Marcus. "Young man, do you know how many kids break their arms and legs from falls just like the one you did there?"

With a shrug Marcus asked, "Any of them ninjas?"

Aunt Rebecca huffed and opened her mouth and I knew a lecture was coming.

"'Bye, Marcus," I called out with a wave. I grabbed Sky's hand and kind of hoped Aunt Rebecca would follow.

With a last nervous glance at Marcus, Aunt Rebecca turned to me. "We'll follow you home so you don't get into any trouble."

The bike ride home was interesting. I got to feel what it was like to be stalked. Aunt Rebecca followed behind me with her hazard lights flashing. There wasn't a lot of traffic, so I tried not to let it bother me. Instead, I thought about Mr. Lee. I kind of felt good about what we were about to do. He'd looked so happy during the speed-dating event when he'd told Ms. HR-Librarian he'd wanted to be a travel writer. But no matter what happened, at least we'd be able to tell Angry Bride that her evil florist has been dealt with. And maybe, when it was all over, Mr. Lee would make a career change and finally try for his dream.

As I rode down the road ahead of Aunt Rebecca I considered what kind of Revenger I wanted Marcus and me to be. I still wanted to get rid of people who were jerks, and making money was one of our very top goals, but maybe we should add another side to our business. One where we helped people too. Ronie's dud of a boyfriend got a record deal because of us, which wasn't at all what we intended, but we were still responsible for it. Our substitute teacher Mr. Schev was running his own business because of us. He was living his dream as well and we'd only been paid for getting rid of him as a teacher. The more I thought about it the more I considered that there was an untapped market here. A way for us to make twice as much money as we were already making. Marcus wasn't going to love the idea and I still needed to consider just how we'd actually pick targets that way, but I could feel the gears spinning in my head and I was excited for it.

"Jared," Aunt Rebecca called from behind me as I glided into the driveway, making me jump and almost fall off my bike. She stepped out of the car. "You really need to pay better attention when you're riding on the street. There were at least half a dozen times where you neglected the rules of the road."

Smile and nod, I told myself. I had to clench my teeth to keep the smile going. I headed into the house. Aunt Rebecca kept talking about road safety. Sky skipped ahead of us into the house. Once inside, Aunt Rebecca finally paused long enough to take a breath. I jumped in, thanked her for making sure I got home safe, and said I was going to bed.

"Don't forget to floss," she called out as I headed up the stairs. "Gingivitis is a killer!"

I briefly thought about wrapping a piece of floss around my neck and acting like I'd somehow strangled myself. It would be funny to see how she reacted to that. But my mom might not be too happy if I gave Aunt Rebecca a heart attack.

Instead I told Sky a bedtime story about a group of rebels who called themselves Revengers who fixed problems for people, using their mad-Revenger-skills to take out jerks and bullies. She made me add a unicorn and a rainbow to the story but I managed to pull it off.

CHAPTER EIGHT

*M*arcus hadn't emailed before I went to bed. When I woke up there weren't any messages from him either. I wondered how long we'd have to wait before APE contacted us. I wondered also if they'd cancel our order if they found out we were way under twenty-one-years old. That thought had me wondering, too, if they might find out we were Revengers. If they could kidnap people in broad daylight, they'd have to have some pretty smart people behind the business and they probably did background checks on their customers. My mind got away from me then and I had visions of news people showing up, and our parents finding out what we'd been up to. My breath shortened and got really fast. My hands started to shake. Aunt Rebecca snapped me out of it by calling out that my mom was on the phone for me.

I ran downstairs so I had a reason to be out of breath when I stepped into the kitchen. Sky was just saying goodbye on the phone. She seemed really excited about something as she handed me the phone.

"Hi, Mom," I said.

"Hi, honey. Listen, Ronie is doing really well and she's advanced to the final round."

"Great." Wherever my mom was calling from it sounded like a party with music and a lot of yelling. I did my best to force my concern about Mr. Lee and the kidnapping out of my head so my mom wouldn't pick up on the fact something was wrong.

Her voice came back on the phone line all bright and cheerful. "We're going to be here another night. We'll be home Sunday for sure."

Another whole day and night and another morning with Aunt Rebecca! Before I had a full-on freak out, I had another thought: maybe my folks *not* coming home was a good thing. Aunt Rebecca didn't know my friends or me for that matter, I might be able to come and go a bit easier without her calling me on my bluffs. I'd still have to deal with her worrying about me every twelve seconds.

"Is everything going okay there?" Mom asked.

Darn it. I'd been too quiet for too long and she'd picked up on it. I put as much energy as I could into my voice. "Oh yeah, it's fine. Tell Ronnie I said to break a leg, or sprain an ankle, knock yourself out on the balance beam or whatever it is you say to gymnasts for them to do well."

"I'll tell her you said good luck," Mom said with a chuckle. "Take care of your sister, okay? We'll see you tomorrow."

I hung up and glanced over at Aunt Rebecca. She and Sky were making pancakes for breakfast. My stomach was way too jumpy for me to eat anything. I would've called Marcus but I didn't want Sky or Aunt Rebecca to listen in on any of our Revenger plans.

"I'm heading over to hang with Marcus today. And do homework together. We have this... this school project."

Aunt Rebecca turned and stared at me. "What? Without breakfast? Do you know why breakfast is the most important meal of the day?" While she dished me up a couple pancakes she launched into a detailed account of how people who eat breakfast are four times less likely to get into an accident during their morning commute. I scarfed the breakfast down, which prompted Rebecca to explain—in too much detail—the importance of chewing each bite of food.

I must've looked disgusted because she came over and put a hand on my forehead. I jerked away, but she shook her head. "You don't feel too warm, but you look ill. Maybe you should go back to bed."

I forked the last bite of food into my mouth. "Aren't beds dangerous? I mean, you've got your bed bugs and bed sores." I held raised my fork in the the air. "Don't even get me started on the suffocation danger of pillows, right?"

She pointed a bony finger at me and nodded. "Wise beyond your years, Jared. You're exactly right. I haven't slept with a pillow since the late nineties. But rest assured, I used my portable UV sanitizer on your bed—all the beds actually— shortly after I arrived."

"Well, I'm sure I'll sleep a lot better knowing you were in my room UVing my bed." I shivered and muttered, "Whatever that means." I glanced at my watch. "Well, I hate to eat and run but I have some homework I need to work on with Marcus today. My mom's pretty strict about getting homework done and not waiting until the last minute."

Aunt Rebecca bit her lip and nodded in a way that made me think of how a hostage might nod if they're being forced to.

She worked for an insurance company, I reminded myself as I cleared my dishes. Clearly my dad was right: seeing all those horrible accidents had obviously destroyed Aunt Rebecca's ability to take risks.

"I want to go see Marcus. I want to see him jump," Sky said, standing on her chair. "He can teach me to jump too!"

Aunt Rebecca patted Sky on the leg, and she sat down again. "Not today, dear."

I turned and headed out of the kitchen. "It's homework, Sky. Boring school stuff with numbers and stuff you don't like. And no ponies or rainbows or anything pink."

"Okaaaaay," she said with a sigh. She turned to our Aunt. "Can we make a pony pancake?"

Aunt Rebecca had her hands full with Sky and hot pancake griddles. I grabbed my school books and stuffed them into my backpack so it really would look like I was doing homework with Marcus—and we probably should so some. But school was due to let out soon for the summer and even the teachers didn't seem to want to do much with books and stuff.

I jumped in the shower and told myself that Aunt Rebecca probably meant well. She wasn't trying to be a jerk, she just thought she was protecting Sky and me— from everything.

After showering and getting dressed, I dragged on a pair of running shoes, shouted goodbye, grabbed my backpack, and ran outside. I hopped on my bike and bolted down the street before my aunt could plaster me with reflective tape again, and rode over to Marcus's house.

His mom opened the door and smiled when she saw me. "Jared! So good to see you. Are you hungry?" Marcus's mom was younger than my parents by like ten years or something. She worked as a marketing director for some cool technology firm, and Marcus said she spent most of her time at a computer. But she looked like she spent most of her time outside. She had tan skin and was slim and never in a rush the way my parents always seemed to be.

The smell of bacon made my stomach growl. I was about to say I was starving, but Marcus came down the hall, hopping on one foot. He got his second shoe pulled on and tapped the screen of his phone. "You're here," he said as if he'd been waiting for me forever. "Good, we have to go."

"Do we?" I leaned in, trying to edge toward the kitchen. I put my hand over my grumbling stomach.

"Marcus, sweetie," his mom said, "I really don't like you rushing around like this. You're eleven, for goodness sake. What possible urgent matter could an eleven-year-old have?"

"A project," he said without a hesitation. "I told you. We have to get it done this weekend and that means we need to head over to the library."

I smiled and tried to look sincere. As far as excuses went *going to the library* was pretty lame. I wasn't sure I'd ever actually been to the city library. Marcus' mom squinted at us and pursed her lips and I had the distinct impression she knew we were lying.

She tugged Marcus' t-shirt straight. "Library? What resource do you need at the library that you don't have on your own computer?"

Marcus glanced at me. I shrugged and pulled a face because I didn't know what to say. He looked at his mom. "Um, the project is on the, uh, city archives."

Impressive, Marcus. Very impressive.

His mom smiled. "How fascinating. You'll let me see it when it's finished, won't you? I am sure it'll be incredible." She hugged him and moved out of the doorway so Marcus could get by. "Have a good day, and have fun tonight," she called after us as we headed toward the street.

Marcus grabbed his bike and I threw a leg over mine. When we were half a block away, I asked, "Why'd your mom tell us to have fun tonight? What's happening tonight?"

"What do you think's happening?" He smiled and handed me an envelope. Inside were two fist-sized stickers that said: APE BODY TAGS.

"Tonight?" I asked.

"Today," Marcus said. "Four-thirty."

"And you're just telling me now?"

"I only just found out that today was the day," Marcus said. I pulled up beside him. "And you told you rmom?"

He shook his head. "What do you think I am? Crazy? Of course I didn't tell her. I told her I was staying over at your place. We discussed this."

I nodded. He was right, but I hadn't anticipated everything happening so quickly "Okay. Okay. This is going to be good. We're really doing this." My stomach twisted suddenly and I stopped. Marcus skidded to a stop beside me.

"What?" he asked.

"*Are* we really doing this?"

"Jared, relax. It's not like we're really kidnapping Mr. Lee. I mean, this is something he should thank us for. Besides," Marcus added, "do you know what this is going to do for our reputation? When I upload video of him getting abducted, people are finally going to lose their minds. The Revengers will be a name people are actually afraid of."

"And that's what we want, right?"

"Of course we do. The goal is money, right? We want that spy training and the only way we're going to get it is if we get paying customers and the only way that'll happen is if we have a reputation people believe in."

I nodded. He had a point. "You're right. What's with the body tags?"

Marcus held one up. "Four-thirty, at the flower shop. I need to have one of these stuck to me, and so does Mr. Lee. It's to make sure they don't grab the wrong person."

"I can see how that would be a bad thing." I pedaled some more and glanced at Marcus. "If we're not in a real rush, why didn't you let me have some breakfast at your place?"

"My mom seemed super suspicious today when I got up. I think she knows we're up to something and I didn't want to give her time to question us."

My empty stomach grumbled another complaint and I muttered, "Yeah, smart thinking." And then I remembered something else. "We have another problem," I said. "My aunt is here for another twenty-four hours. We need a plan for how to deal with her."

CHAPTER NINE

*M*arcus and I talked it over and decided we'd really go to the library for part of the day. If his mom really was suspicious, she might check on us, or ask Marcus a question about the library that he'd only know the answer to if he had actually been there. Plus, we had to kill time somewhere, and the library was a good a place as any. I called Aunt Rebecca when we got there and to my surprise she didn't mention any library-specific dangers. Aside from maybe getting a papercut from a super old book, I couldn't think of anything dangerous we could run in to at the library either. At least, I didn't, until I ended the call with my aunt and heard a familiar voice behind me that sent a shiver crawling up my spine.

"Marcus and Jared."

Marcus groaned and we turned around together. "Janet," Marcus and I said at the same time.

There was something odd about Janet Everton being at the library at the same time as us, but then again, she did know the answer to pretty much every question in class, and maybe that was because she came here and read everything on the shelves. Still, I couldn't shake the feeling she had somehow followed us there.

"What brings you two to the library?" Before we could answer she added, "Wait, did you know this was a library?" she grimaced. "There are books in there, guys. Books with words you actually have to read. But listen, there is one section on the first floor that has books with lots of pictures. That's where you'll want to go." She smiled sweetly. "Would you like me to show you?"

As annoying as the girl could be, I had to admit her insults were pretty funny. In some other dimension I bet the three of us were friends.

But not this dimension. In this dimension Janet was the enemy and Marcus and I decided a while back to be extra cautious of her. She'd already accused us of being the Revengers. She was right, of course, but we couldn't let her know that.

Marcus folded his arms. "Thanks, Janet. But I think we're good. But listen, you don't have to follow us around you know. If you want to declare your undying love for me, or Jared, just do it. The feeling's totally mutual."

He bat his eyes at her and Janet shook her head and turned about face and headed to a cart of books near the librarian's desk.

Turning to me, Marcus hissed, "We have to do something about her."

I shook my head. "We already had one close call with her on our first job when we captured Evil Cat. If we go after her she's going to start putting it all together and figure us out. So let's just ignore her."

Marcus blew a breath out of his nose. "That's like saying ignore a hurricane."

I agreed but we had to get back to our cover. We both got library cards and used the library's computers, and since we didn't want to do anything that would make anyone think we were the Revengers we watched videos on YouTube. We also got bored enough that we really did our homework. We considered actually writing a fake report on library archives to show Marcus' mom, but decided doing fake homework was very un-Revenger-like. Marcus did ask the librarian to see the archives and he snapped a few pictures, which he said would be enough to show his mom.

By two o'clock we were done our homework and had seen all the YouTube videos we wanted to see. Plus, we were both starving. We left Janet to her stack of books. She watched us leave and I hoped she wouldn't follow. We didn't have to go far. A guy had parked his taco truck just outside the park near the library. We took our bikes over and bought two tacos each and ice-cold lemonade. Sitting on shady grass near the swings, we ate.

Marcus didn't seem all that hungry. He even gave me one of his tacos to eat. He could hardly take a bite, and he kept jumping at every noise. I couldn't blame him, I guess. Every minute brought him closer to his abduction. He wasn't nervous so much as excited. Heck, I wasn't getting kidnapped and every part of my skin buzzed. We hung out at the park, talking about how amazing this was going to be. Just as we were ready to get up and take off for Mr. Lee's, I heard Sky's voice beside me. "Hi, Jared."

I jumped to my feet. So did Marcus. Glancing around, I didn't see Aunt Rebecca. I kneeled eye to eye with Sky. "What are you doing here?"

"I wanted to play on the swings. But now I want to go home. Can you take me?"

"Did Aunt Rebecca bring you?"

She stuck out her lower lip. "I told her I wanted to go, but she said no. I think she's afraid of swings. Now I want you to walk me home."

"Wait, you just walked all the way here? Alone?" We were at least a couple miles from home. No way had Sky walked the whole way by herself. I spun around and scanned the streets for my aunt, who I assumed would be running around in circles, shrieking like a maniac.

I turned back to my sister. "Seriously, Sky, how did you get here?"

Sky crossed her arms over her chest and didn't speak.

"Your sister walked all the way over here?" Marcus asked. He sounded impressed.

I shook my head and turned around again. "It would take her an hour to walk here, and if my aunt has been looking for Sky for an hour she'd have called the neighborhood watch, the police, and the Army Reserve. We'd hear sirens."

I stood and turned to Marcus. "I need your phone."

I didn't remember my aunt's number but called my house and no one picked up. I left a message that we had Sky and that we'd bring her home as well as Marcus' number so she could call us back. As I handed the phone back to Marcus

I had a sick feeling that Sky running away from my Aunt was going to complicate our plan with Mr. Lee.

"Jared, c'mon, there's no time." Marcus glanced at his cell phone. "We need to get to the shop and set up cameras so we can get some video to upload. And we have got to get that body... I mean that tag on Flower Man."

I blew out a breath. The flower shop was kind of on the way home and wasn't that far from the library. But there was no way we could get Sky home and back to Mr. Lee's shop before our deadline. "She has to come with us," I said.

Sky clapped excitedly.

"There's a bookstore right beside the flower shop," Marcus said quietly so Sky wouldn't hear. "Just bring Sky, put her in front of some pony books, we deal with all our stuff, and then you can take her home."

I hated the idea of Sky being anywhere near this. I mean, I had no idea how APE was going to abduct Marcus and Mr. Lee. If they were going to make it real, it might not be something for a six-year-old to see. But if I put her in the bookstore, that might work.

What option did I have?

None.

Our plan was in motion. We couldn't pull the plug at this point or we'd forfeit our deposit. I wasn't going to waste all our hard earned cash.

I nodded and took my sister's hand. "Sky, we're going to a bookstore first. I'll call Aunt Rebecca again and hope to reach her so she doesn't freak out." I put my bike helmet on Sky and lifted her onto the bike seat. "Hold on tight."

She giggled. It wasn't the first time we'd doubled. I took her on rides all the time. I imagined if Aunt Rebecca could see us she'd lose her mind, but I was pretty sure she was already losing her mind. I felt kinda bad for her too, because losing a kid has got to be pretty scary for an adult.

Straight home after the abduction, I told myself. Maybe Rebecca would be happy I found Sky. I might be the hero. I held onto that thought even though I was pretty sure it was all wishful thinking.

Sky wrapped her arms around my waist and we took off with Marcus leading the way. We made it to the flower shop a few minutes later, which was pretty good time considering Sky was on the back and I couldn't go as fast as my usual speed. Marcus checked his phone. We had a solid fifteen minutes before the APE kidnappers showed up.

I took Sky into the bookstore beside the flower shop and plunked her in the middle of a nest of books about ponies and fairies. She sat there, turning pages, touching every pony drawing. From where she sat I could see through the front windows to the sidewalk where Marcus stood. He checked the time on his phone, shifting his weight from one foot to the next and rolling his neck like he was a boxer gearing up for the main event.

When I stepped outside again, I glanced back. I could easily see Sky happily leafing through the pages.

We were doing this. We were actually doing this. I walked over to Marcus and felt my heart pounding faster and faster with each step. "You ready for this?"

"Are you kidding?" If his grin went any wider, his face would split in half. "I have never been more ready for anything in my entire life. Do you think I'm supposed to struggle? Do I fight them off at all? They said they want the experience to be as real as possible."

I laughed. "Just try not to jump into their arms giggling like my sister. Mr. Lee might not buy it's a real kidnapping if you do that."

He nodded. "Good point."

I imagined how that would look. Marcus running up the kidnappers and hugging them while any illusion of it being real shattered. I laughed at the image.

I shook my head and glanced into the flower shop. "Do we have a plan to get Flower Man outside? Do we need him to be outside? Or will the APE guys take care of that?"

"Huh?" Marcus turned and looked at the flower shop. "Oh, yeah, right. I don't know. Whatever you think."

Mr. Lee had barrels of wilting flowers out front. Most of them looked half dead from the heat, but there were so many different kinds I thought it would be pretty normal to ask for help picking out specific ones. Didn't hurt to help the APEs.

"How much time do we have?" I asked.

Marcus glanced at his cell phone. "Five minutes. You don't think we missed them do you?"

I shook my head. "For the money we paid them, I think they'll come right on time. But we better get Mr. Lee out here."

Marcus opened the front door and called, "Excuse me, Sir, could we get a bit of help out here?"

Mr. Lee had on a white, short-sleeved dress shirt and khaki pants. He smiled when he stepped outside. "I've seen you boys around here, haven't I?"

"We, um, don't live too far from here," Marcus said. "We pass by your shop all the time. Totally normal and unremarkable for us to be here right now." He laughed nervously and twitched. "Just a couple of regular guys, looking for flowers. Nothing odd about that, right."

Mr Lee's expression turned to puzzled, but just for a moment. He wiped a cloth across his forehead and turned to the barrels of flowers. "What can I help you two with?"

While Marcus spoke with Mr. Lee, a black van turned the corner and parked just down the street. Dark, tinted windows wouldn't let me see the driver, or if anyone else was inside. It had to be them.

I turned to Marcus and wiggled my eyebrows. He nodded back.

And then a shrill voice cracked out at me. "Jared!"

I jerked around to see Aunt Rebecca sprinting like a wild animal from the other end of the street toward me.

"Oh, great," I said to Marcus. With Aunt Rebecca rushing toward us, that meant one thing—our thousand-dollar plan was about to be ruined.

Busted once again.

CHAPTER TEN

"*H*ave you seen your sister?" The words tumbled out of her mouth as a single, panicked word and her eyes were like giant pieces of glass, wide with horror. Her face was streaked from either tears or sweat or both. She grabbed me by my shoulders and shook me. "Do you know where she is?" Panic shook her voice. "Jared, please, tell me you know where Sky is. I can't find her. I took her to the park and turned around for a second and she was gone. Just—" her voice cracked and tears filled her eyes.

I'd never seen someone so broken. So horrified. Shame washed over me for not doing more to get in touch with her, and let her know I'd found Sky. I blinked and found myself a second. "Yeah. Yes. I have her—I mean, we found her. I called and left a message."

Her whole body seemed to sag with relief and she let out a huge breath and I felt the weight of her as she leaned against me. "Oh, thank everything. Where is she?"

I pointed to the bookstore. I could still see Sky sitting in her pile of books where I'd left her.

Rebecca turned and smiled and looked up at the sky and muttered something, a prayer no doubt. "Why didn't you try to find me at the park?" She asked turning back to me. "I was frantic, Jared. Absolutely frantic."

"Aunt Rebecca, I called you. And when I couldn't see you I decided to take Sky home. She wanted to stop to read a book, and we were about to call you again." I turned to Marcus. "Right, Marcus? We were about to call her again."

"Totally," he said.

Her face reddened. Beads of sweat dripped down her face.

"Pardon me," Mr. Lee said, stepping a bit closer. I'd forgotten about him. He looked from me to Aunt Rebecca. "Is everything okay here?"

Aunt Rebecca nodded. "It is now. Just a family discussion!"

I rolled my eyes and turned to the florist. "Sorry, sir. This is my aunt. She was worried about my little sister."

He glanced at me, his eyes narrowed like he was trying to remember where or if he'd seen me before. I realized then that we should have been more careful about staying unnoticed by him. I kept thinking how close we'd sat to him at the minute-man dating thing.

Marcus pushed out his hand to Aunt Rebecca. He took her hand and shook it. "Hi, Jared's Aunt Rebecca. I'm Jared's friend, Marcus. We met yesterday, remember?" He pulled her toward Mr. Lee. "And this is Mr. Lee. This is his flower shop."

Aunt Rebecca blinked and Mr. Lee's mouth fell open

with what looked like surprise. Marcus put his hand on Aunt Rebecca's back and urged her toward Mr. Lee. Stepping back, Marcus swiped a finger across his phone's screen.

Pulling herself together, Aunt Rebecca faced Mr. Lee. "I am sorry for the scene. Their parents are out of the city and taking care of kids isn't something I do too often these days. I'm afraid I'm not much of a babysitter."

"I totally understand," Mr. Lee said, taking her hand and patting it.

A sudden screech of tires interrupted from down the street and a second later the black van up skidded to a stop beside us. Dust and burned rubber swirled around us. The side door slid open. Four men jumped out, all of them wearing black ski masks. Two men grabbed Mr. Lee by his arms.

"Hey!" he shouted. "What's going on?"

They swept him off his feet and tossed him into the van. Aunt Rebecca let out a screech. I was sure that when she saw these guys grab Marcus, she'd lose it entirely. I'd have to tell her everything. I'd have to tell the police the truth too, if they showed up. And I was willing to bet they would because Aunt Rebecca called 9-1-1 when a car ran a red light. I wasn't looking forward to a huge freak out, not to mention possible jail time.

But instead of grabbing Marcus, the guys in black grabbed Aunt Rebecca.

"No!" she screamed.

Mouth open, I stood there. I didn't know what to do.

One man grabbed Aunt Rebecca by her shoulders and the second man went for her legs. Aunt Rebecca wasn't standing for any of it—literally. Her foot shot out like a ninja and connected with the man's face, sending him back into the van. Aunt Rebecca stomped on the foot of the man who had her shoulders. He swore and his grip loosened. Rebecca spun and punched the man right in the throat. He stumbled against the side of the van, gasping and sputtering. The other two men in masks, the ones who had grabbed Mr. Lee, jumped out. Aunt Rebecca didn't get a chance to land another punch. The first man had recovered too so it was three against one, and my aunt didn't have a chance. They picked her right off the ground and shoved her into the van.

She thrashed, punched, and kicked. I watched her, a little afraid of her and for her. I felt bad for how frightened she looked, but boy could she fight. I should have done something to help her but I was mesmerized by her ability to kick butt. She twisted and I caught a glimpse of her back. The APE body tag flapped in the breeze. The guys jumped in the van, the door slammed, and the van took off.

We stood there a moment, silent while the dust and weight of what had just happened settled around us.

Finally, I turned to Marcus. "What the—? What did you do?"

CHAPTER ELEVEN

"Seriously, Marcus," I said. "What just happened?"

Marcus didn't look at me. He kept his phone pointed at the van as it sped away. He'd recorded the whole thing.

Once the van had disappeared around the corner, Marcus put his phone down. "Sorry. I mean, I really wanted to go, but she was losing it. And if they'd have left with me you know she'd have called the police and our Revenger days would be over."

I'd come to the same conclusion but still, her getting abducted only delayed the inevitable.

"Besides," Marcus added, "if ever there was a person who needed to be tied to a chair for a couple days, it's that woman, am I right?"

I pressed my hands to the side of my head. All I could think was how mad my parents were going to be if they found out I was behind Aunt Rebecca's abduction. I'd taken out my babysitter! I'd had mom's friend kidnapped. I was dead meat.

Marcus must've read my mind because he said, "Relax. No one's going to know it was us."

"I can't believe you put the tag on her. How do we get her back?"

Marcus shook his head. "Man, can you imagine what she would have done if I'd been taken? She'd have called the cops, my parents, the fire department, and who knows who else. We'd have been tagged as Revengers for sure." He shook his head. "This is better."

"She's going to die of fright. I mean seriously, she's going to physically die. We shouldn't have done this!"

Marcus rolled his eyes. "Give me a break. They're not real kidnappers. If she gets crazy frightened, they'll tell her the truth. If her health is in any kind of danger, they'll take her to the hospital. They're not real bad guys. They're an entertainment business. A mobile theme park with a little extra theme."

I felt a bit better hearing Marcus say that. My shoulders eased down, but my heart was still hammering. I glanced back through the window into the bookstore. Sky still sat in her pile of books, smiling and turning pages. I turned in a circle to see if anyone else was freaking out about two people being forced into a black van in broad daylight. I didn't see anyone else on the street. A couple holding hands turned the corner and stopped to admire a window display.

Glancing at Mr. Lee's shop, I told Marcus. "We need to put up the closed sign."

Once we'd turned the sign around and closed the door to his shop, Marcus blew out a breath. "When I stop being super disappointed that I missed out on one of the greatest opportunities to experience something awesome, why don't we go back to your place. APE is supposed to email us a link so we can watch streaming footage of Mr. Lee and your babysitter getting everything a thousand dollars buys." He shook his head. "A thousand dollars and I didn't even get to be part of it."

I couldn't believe no one had seen the kidnapping. I glanced around again and noticed half a dozen pieces of paper on the ground. I picked it up and saw the APE logo.

YOU HAVE JUST WITNESSED ABDUCTION BY ADVENTURE PLUS ENTERPRISES.

The paper listed a phone number you could call if you had any questions. A note to law enforcement said that if they happened to respond they could make inquiries at a specific address.

Marcus pushed out his fist. "Well, partner, another mission accomplished."

I bumped my fist into his, but I wasn't sure everything had gone as planned. Eventually, APE would tell Aunt Rebecca and Mr. Lee that someone had signed them up for this experience. I wasn't sure what would happen after that.

Marcus and I could still end up in juvenile detention.

"You got to admit," Marcus said as we headed to get Sky and our bikes, "that was the coolest thing you've seen in a very long time, right? I mean, it was almost better than watching the INS come and arrest Shevchenko. And way better than seeing Gunnar get his record contract after we bought him a bus ticket to Los Angeles."

I nodded. "Yeah, way better. But my parents come home tomorrow. What am I going to tell them?"

"Do you think they'd believe she ran away with a florist?"

I shook my head. "No. And what about when she shows up on our doorstep all freaked out, asking why we didn't call the police?"

Marcus held up the paper the kidnappers had left behind. "We say we figured she—or Mr. Lee—had purchased this adventure and we hoped she'd have fun."

"That could work. After all, we're just a couple of stupid eleven-year-olds."

"Speak for yourself," Marcus said.

Sky knocked on the window of the bookshop and waved, holding up a copy of a book with a big dog on the cover. I could see I'd better buy her a book or face more pouting lips.

Watching Sky, Marcus said, "Of course, this means you're the only babysitter around for the next twenty-four hours."

I looked at him. "What do you mean *I'm* the only babysitter? You already told your mom you're sleeping over tonight. So looks like we're both babysitting."

After a dinner of frozen pizza, I read to Sky the big dog mystery book five times until she finally fell asleep on the couch. I carried her to bed, took off her shoes, and tucked her in with her favorite stuffed pony.

Mom called and I made it sound like we were watching a movie and couldn't talk because we'd just gotten to the really exciting dragon part. I told her everything was good. I heard Ronie chattering in the background so I had a feeling Mom had her hands full too. She didn't even ask about Aunt Rebecca, so I didn't have to lie and the whole call took maybe thirty seconds.

As I plopped back down on the couch, I saw Marcus watching the video he'd shot. "Did you see the way your babysitter fought today?"

"I know. Talk about crazy! She was practically a ninja out there. Maybe you can lend her your outfit."

"Or put her into the WWE." Marcus started tapping the screen on his tablet over and over.

"What are you doing?" I asked.

"Hmm? Oh, refreshing my email. Remember, the APE is supposed to send us a link to see what's happening with the kidnapping. It's totally late."

"I'm sure it'll show up."

"Well, you pay a thousand dollars for something, you expect them to be reliable. I mean, how hard is it to send a link?"

We ended up watching a couple of movies and finally went to sleep way after midnight. APE still hadn't sent the link, and Marcus fired off an email asking where it was. I couldn't help but think that maybe no news was bad news. Maybe Aunt Rebecca had managed to take out her kidnappers. Then what would we do?

CHAPTER TWELVE

I woke up to Marcus shaking me and yelling, "Get up!"

I shot out of bed, stumbled over a blanket, and glanced around. "What? What's wrong? Is Sky okay?"

Marcus let out a frustrated breath and shook his head. "This is not about Sky. She's still asleep." He held up his tablet. "APE sent a link. You have to see what happened."

I rubbed my eyes and settled on the edge of my bed. Marcus handed me his tablet. When I didn't start the video fast enough, he reached down and tapped the screen.

A warehouse appeared. Dirty ground, a few piles of broken lumber, dim light—yeah, looked like a warehouse to me. Exposed pipes, beams, and sheet metal made up the walls. Light suddenly flooded the room, some of it from overhead lights, but most of it came from an open skylight. Some parts of the walls and ceiling were missing.

The camera focused and I saw Mr. Lee and Aunt Rebecca sitting on straight wooden chairs, their hands tied behind them, their chairs placed back to back. Blindfolds covered the top parts of their faces.

I glanced at Marcus. "Whoa, they went all out. And to think that was almost you."

He gestured back to the screen. "Just watch, man. Just watch."

My stomach twisted and I sat up straighter.

"What do you want?" Mr. Lee asked. "Who's there?"

"I can hear them breathing," Aunt Rebecca whispered.

"Who are you?" Mr. Lee called out again. "What do you want with us? I am sure you have the wrong people. If you just let us explain who we are, I think you'll see—"

"Quiet!" The voice came from off screen, but two men walked over and pulled off the blindfolds.

"Who are you?" Aunt Rebecca demanded. To her credit, she didn't sound frightened. She sounded angry, like she was getting ready to punch someone again. I wondered if this had rattled something free inside her. I almost didn't know her as my too-scared babysitter.

"You know what," Marcus said, "you can watch the whole thing later." He leaned over and tapped the screen and the image jumped ahead a couple hours. The kidnappers had left the room. Mr. Lee and Aunt Rebecca rocked back and forth on their chairs. "This was your babysitter's idea," Marcus said. He pointed at the screen. "Watch."

Aunt Rebecca rocked her chair and managed to get onto her toes. I didn't see how that could possibly help as rope still held her chest to the chair. It looked like her arms had been tied to the chair arms and her legs to the chair legs. Still, she was doing some impressive balancing. Then she did something that really surprised me. She managed a small jump and spun hard. She went down on her side but the side of the chair smashed against the ground. The arm broke off. Part of the back of the chair broke with a crack. A couple seconds of thrashing and Aunt Rebecca stood, a piece of broken chair still strapped to her leg.

She must've heard something because she kicked the chair leg, got free, and ducked behind one of the piles of scrap lumber. A man in a ski mask came in. He bent down over the broken chair and swore.

Getting up he brought his face right up into Mr. Lee's face. "Where is she?"

Aunt Rebecca stepped out from behind the scrap wood, a large board in her hands.

Mr. Lee jerked forward suddenly and struck his head into the kidnapper's face. The kidnapper staggered back. Aunt Rebecca stepped up and clobbered him with the wood. It hit with a solid whack, and I winched.

I couldn't believe what I was seeing. I glanced at Marcus. He had one hand to the side of his head like he'd been hit with that board. When I looked back at the video, Aunt Rebecca had freed Mr. Lee. They glanced around, grabbed hands, and ran, disappearing off the view of the camera.

"When did this happen?" I asked.

Marcus picked up the tablet and tapped the screen again. He brought up an email from APE. It was short. They said they were sorry for failing to give full value and so were giving a full refund. It was really nice, but basically it said don't call us again.

"Seriously," Marcus said, "your babysitter has major guts."

"Wait!" I turned on the bed and rubbed my eyes. "If they escaped, and if APE gave our money back, that means Aunt Rebecca and Mr. Lee are free. And that means—"

Downstairs the front door opened and slammed closed.

Marcus clutched his tablet to his chest. "Ooops."

CHAPTER THIRTEEN

"*J*ust be cool about it," Marcus kept saying. "Remember, we saw the pamphlet. We thought they'd paid for some kind of adventure."

We came down the stairs slow, peering around, hoping we wouldn't be facing a babysitter who could probably kick both of our butts. We found Aunt Rebecca in the kitchen, making a pot of coffee. Mr. Lee sat at the table, watching her contentedly. They both looked a little rumpled, but also about ten years younger.

"You're... um... you're back," I said. "How was your, uh, kidnapping?"

"You know about it?" Aunt Rebecca turned from the stove and put a stare on me that felt like a sharp stick.

Marcus handed her the note that APE had left at the not-really-a-crime scene. "The people who took you left this."

Aunt Rebecca snatched up the paper. She glanced at it and handed it to Mr. Lee. He frowned at it, turned it over, and seemed to read each and every word twice.

"How is Sky?" Aunt Rebecca asked.

"She's fine," I said. "Sleeping in her room."

"We looked them up online," Marcus said about APE. "It must've been an amazing experience."

"Yeah." I wet my lips and tried really hard to sound like someone dying to know more, and not someone totally guilty. "Why didn't you tell us you were doing such a wild thing?"

Aunt Rebecca smiled. She poured herself a cup of coffee and laughed. She laughed louder and Mr. Lee started laughing too.

Marcus and I looked at each other. I wondered if Mr. Lee and Aunt Rebecca might be having some kind of post-traumatic stress. Maybe they were even on the verge of a total meltdown.

"We didn't know it was fake, until after we'd escaped." Aunt Rebecca said, still laughing.

"One of the most frightening things I've been through," Mr. Lee said, leaning back in his chair. "And exhilarating."

Aunt Rebecca took a sip of her coffee. "You did really good taking care of your sister, Jared." She gestured to the kitchen. "And the place looks good even though you two—you three," she added, gesturing to Marcus, "—were on your own all night."

"Um," I swallowed and glanced around. "Thank you... I guess."

"Your parents will be home tonight, and I think you're going to be just fine watching your sister on your own today."

My jaw went slack. I felt my eyes widen. "Where will you be?"

Mr. Lee smiled. "The experience was... illuminating."

"To say the least." Aunt Rebecca nodded. "I not only survived. I rose to meet the challenge head on." She punched the air. Marcus ducked even though he was nowhere near her.

I chewed my lower lip. I had to ask, "So... you're not worried about sharp edges anymore? Or electrical outlets? Or metal utensils? Falling books?"

She laughed and held up her hand. "Jared, you can't live a life that is only a reaction to the accidents of others. Those weren't my accidents. I think I forgot I needed just a touch of risk to really feel alive."

Reaching out, Mr. Lee took Aunt Rebecca's hand. "I've been wanting to see the ruins of Angkor Wat all my life and I've put it off long enough."

"We've both put off too much, Andrew."

I looked at Marcus and he shrugged. I knew he didn't have a clue where or what Angkor Wat was.

Aunt Rebecca must have seen our blank stares. "That's Cambodia, boys. I've always wanted to be someone who travels, but I was scared stupid about flying." She sipped her coffee again. "I'm still scared stupid about flying, I suppose, but I think the two of us make a pretty good team."

"No argument from me," Mr. Lee said, grinning. He let go of her hand.

Aunt Rebecca put her cup in the sink. "I'll be right back. I'm just going to grab my things."

When she left, Mr. Lee leaned forward. "Didn't you boys come into my shop the day that sprinkler head malfunctioned? You bought an orchid. And then I saw you afterwards when the fire department was there."

I blinked, but didn't say anything. What could I say?

"And I went to a speed dating event at the rec center not too long ago. You two were there, sitting at a table nearby. Eating French fries if I recall."

My mouth dried up. "Uh, it's a small town?"

"Not that small." He looked from Marcus to me and back again. "What did I do to you guys?"

I was about to deny everything, tell the guy I didn't know what he was talking about, but for some reason I got the feeling he wasn't mad. Just curious. It felt right to tell him. I put up my chin and said, "You delivered dead flowers to a wedding. And you asked for it."

Marcus groaned.

Mr. Lee sat back as if he hadn't thought I'd tell him the truth. "Ah, yes, the McKenzie-Everton wedding. Partly that was my fault. Partly it was my brother's idiot son and this heat wave. They ordered Japanese water lilies, and those need to be kept wet or they die about ten times faster than roses. I told my nephew to keep them in water. He forgot. The heat just did the rest." He eyed us. "How did you know about that?"

"Don't tell him," Marcus whispered, but not so quietly that Mr. Lee couldn't hear.

I shook my head. "He deserves to know. Deloris, the bride, hired us to make you pay for it. We wouldn't have taken the job except you hired us too. And then during your speed-date you said you wanted to be a travel writer. We thought we could make it happen, so you'd be happy, and Angry Bride would be happy too."

"His Aunt Rebecca wasn't supposed to be part of it," Marcus said. "I was supposed to be."

Mr. Lee sat up. "You?"

"Well, yeah. Do you know how cool that looked when you guys were taken? I would have loved it."

Mr. Lee shook his head. "I'll apologize again to Ms. Everton who is now Mrs. McKenzie. But she didn't seem all that upset at the wedding. Her niece, on the other hand, seemed very angry." He shook his head. "I can't believe a couple kids like you have a revenge business."

"Not revenge... not really. And you won't tell anyone, will you?" I asked.

"I wouldn't dare! I'd hate to see what you might do if someone actually did something to the two of you."

I looked at Marcus and smiled. He was struggling not to laugh. I knew he was thinking the same thing as me— Mr. Shevchenko, our very mean, candy-stealing, deported substitute teacher. He'd learned better than to cross us.

Mr. Lee stood up. "Besides, I must thank you instead. You set me off on an adventure that I've always wanted but didn't know where to begin. You've killed the old Mr. Lee, the flower man. I'm now a new Mr. Lee who is ready to take on a new life!"

Aunt Rebecca walked into the kitchen, carrying her duffle bag. She tossed her bubble wrap on the table. "Have fun popping it. You'll say goodbye to Sky for me?"

"You bet. I mean, of course I will." I couldn't hide the relief that she'd be leaving before my parents got home. Leaving and heading far away with Mr. Lee. I was happy for her—and Mr. Lee. But even more I was glad that Aunt Rebecca might not be around for any more babysitting jobs.

"I'll bring you kids something back from Cambodia."

She gave me a hug. Marcus held out his hand for a shake, but she pulled him into a hug too. He made a face over that. Hand in hand, the babysitter and the florist walked out the door. I wasn't sure we'd see them again.

CHAPTER FOURTEEN

My parents came home happy and tired. Mom seemed a little surprised that Aunt Rebecca had left so early, but when I told her Rebecca had met someone her mood changed in an instant.

"I'm so glad," my mom said. "She's been alone for too many years."

Ronie took first place in every one of her categories, so she was all grins and didn't even ruffle my hair. On Monday, Marcus and I walked to school with smug smiles. We'd uploaded the kidnapping video. Views had gone up a thousand percent. We hadn't accepted any other admissions, but the emails rolled in by the dozens.

Because of the refund from APE, Marcus and I had our money back.

I did have one thing bugging me. I kept looking over my shoulder. I couldn't put my finger on what was wrong until we walked into class and I saw Janet sitting with a bunch of girls, scrolling through pictures on her phone.

That's when the realization of what had happened came crashing down and I suddenly felt as if I'd been kicked in the stomach by a karate expert.

Marcus groaned and nodded in Janet's direction. "Trouble at ten o'clock."

I grabbed his arm and pulled him away from Janet and her friends.

"Whoa, what?" he said. He must've seen the horror in my face because he added, "Seriously, what's wrong? Are you sick?"

"I might be," I said. I took a couple slow breaths. "Janet" I spoke her name like it was the clue we'd been searching for and Marcus gave me a confused look. "As in Janet Everton."

Marcus shrugged and then his mouth dropped as he realized the same thing I'd realized. "Angry bride's last name was Everton before she got married."

I nodded. "And Mr. Lee said it had been Angry Bride's niece was the one upset about the dead flowers."

We took a second to let the weight of what Janet had pulled over on us and then headed for the back of the classroom in silence. We didn't make it.

Janet stopped us in the hall just outside the classroom with a couple of her friends. She smiled. A scary smile. Like she knew something—which I was pretty sure she did. "I was just thinking about you two. Have you seen the Revengers website lately?"

"Who hasn't?" Jennifer, one of Janet's best friends, said. "I love that site."

Thank you, Jennifer, I thought.

But Janet kept talking. "Well, funny story. My aunt got married last week and her florist is the latest hit by the Revengers." She eyed us each carefully. "Weird, hey?"

I swallowed. "Yeah, weird. Only maybe not so much. Sounds like they got a good target."

"Yeah. Totally," Marcus said nodding.

Smiling, Janet turned back to her friends. She scrolled through another photo on her phone. When she looked up, she nodded at us.

All the places we'd run into her hadn't been by chance at all. She'd followed us. She was like some creepy, but actually kind of brilliant mastermind-stalker.

She knew. She totally knew. She'd been the one to send us the email. She'd pretended to be her aunt. She'd sent us that job, probably just to see if we'd take it so she could prove to herself that we were the ones.

Now the school's biggest gossip knew we were the Revengers. The question was—what would she do about it?

Maybe nothing. Maybe she wanted to keep hiring us.

Or maybe this was just the beginning of what would be a lot of trouble.

I straightened and clenched my teeth. If Janet Everton wanted trouble that was fine with me. It didn't matter. We were Revengers. We knew how to deal with trouble.

THE END

READ THE SERIES
BE PART
OF THE MAYHEM!

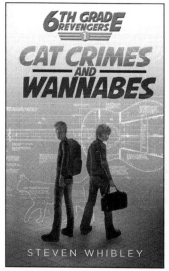

6TH GRADE REVENGERS
3

A
GAME
OF
THORNS

Hotel

STEVEN WHIBLEY

6TH GRADE REVENGERS
4

CINEPHILES
AND
HAMSTER
HUNTERS

STEVEN WHIBLEY

6TH GRADE REVENGERS
5

SUPER
TROOPER

STEVEN WHIBLEY

If you liked this book,
check out these other books
by STEVEN WHIBLEY

ABOUT THE AUTHOR

Steven Whibley is the author of several middle grade and young adult novels. He lives in British Columbia with his wife and two (soon to be three) young children. If you would like to connect with Steven, please check out his website at www.StevenWhibley.com

Made in the USA
Middletown, DE
06 March 2019